ADELAIDE JARNOT

Trails
to the
Canyon Floor

Trails to the Canyon Floor
by ADELAIDE JARNOT

Cover Art by **Evangeline Knight**
Author Photo by **Max Wolfe**

MYSTIC BOXING COMMISSION

ISBN#: 979-8-9905623-7-0
1st Print: June 2025 — Mystic Boxing Commission, Los Angeles, CA

TRAILWAYS OF CONTENTS

TRAILWAYS OF CONTENTS

WE FLEW TOGETHER TO LIVE ON THE MOON

My fingertips calloused from thick textured rings
Thickened from sliding up and down guitar strings.
We melt in a sea of warm lavender cream
As I drift into sleep, into velvet dreams:

At a vine covered café, they are meeting at Noon
And soon flew together to live on the moon.
As I read to you, candles burn into sickle cells
And can't carry the weight of the gone lovers' dell.

I wake from my slumber in closed silken seams
As air cultivates our valley with magic streams.
At a cast-iron table, I'm looking at you
While our decision is made, and our repast through:

Iced tea, a lemon wedge,
Toast with jam, a crusted edge;
And in the scalding sun of that valley noon,
We flew together to live on the moon.

THE DEVIL'S DARNING NEEDLES

Beetlebum the ice-cream man
with his ties and tethers
and leathery hands
escapes into bitter, fruitless lands
    unsuccessful in completing
    the will of God

Beetles and gnats and cold evil creatures;
bold freaks of nature
to hold in their places –
a burden so steadfast
    it couldn't escape a hole
    if it tried

A lake, or a pond, or so mutable a land
                of sucrose;
Courageous hole of *pothos*
Grows behind that blue door

The Devil's darning needles adorn
frostbitten wooden beetles
who come to sew your mouth shut
and slice out your eyes

Silly little dragonfly pulls out the ball of
one of your eyes
snip

    snip

       snip

         snipping
        at the membrane
        connecting to your head

Oh, the Devil's darning needles
function like speaking to *bespittle*
   (upon delicate anatomy of the great
   French Queen)
but not to be rude,
and certainly, not to be mean,
But the Devil's darning needles
   will surely snatch you
   in your sleep

About 3,000 coming down from Southlands
to reach hands— *Tarsus*—into your
watery little eyes

And when the beetles come to take you,
   making you into their new home,
cockroaches lodged between your ribs,
   with worms in the notches of your spine,

Just know,
you will see where God's great *Devine* lies,
   because the Devil's darning needles
   have taken your eyes.

CARVING PROJECT

In the boredom crack of dawn,
Submerged in such a ravine;
   Field dressing on the hay
Finds the means
     With which to be seen.

Bleating at each other
In the eyes of those forgone;
From splendid eyes a-plenty
Beady eyes of a fawn.

Blowing until the broadside
Amidst a sea of evergreens,
Button buck is busted by
Cross-stitched twine seams.

Quartering the excess,
Entrails ebbing between the grass;
Quickly paced and softly spoken
A horrid whistle of solid brass.

In golden lands a buster's broken
Until the beats of blood suffice
   In sun-kissed lands of honor,
In holes occupied by mice.

RIPPLES IN PIGMENT

Sweet-smelling wine
On the last summer's day.

Roses a-bloom in this garden.
Golden sunlight filtering
      through window shades.

A jar of olives on a kitchen table.
A haunted forest creeping into
               the yard.

This house, manifesting a grave.

THE BOY WHO MADE THE WORLD END

I was sickened in my cell,
when out of the covers, a darling spell
bewitched me into pearl-encrusted cases,
bringing me out of old hidden places.

Then there he was, this darling boy; his hair
                    Brighter than reflection
from his diamond, pearl, and amethyst necklace.
His eyes, could tell you a thousand secrets,
                    Before blinking half-twice;

As he rode a carriage of giant mice,
The blood of a newborn should surely suffice;
for he spared, as he spared, so he spared all their lives,
robbing ill-conceived thieves, his own Robin Hood.

Would I dare tell you more? Well, I probably should,
as his voice was as smooth as a carpenter's wood.
The chambers of your heart would pulse like
                          earthquake.
Whenever he spoke your name.

His body flowed in smooth windy whirls
as he embodied the grace of boyhood "church" murals.
It's in the way he came soaring which would
                          make you unfurl.
For him, they were willing to die.

He'd figure 8, in one impetuous twirl,
And your secrets would burst as your arteries swirled.
The squeezing inside might just make you hurl
And that's how this darling boy ended the world.

Yes, he marched right on with his wide heavy drum,
beating the beats of destruction to come.
Creating a crack in the wide heavy ground
it was louder than ever had been heard any sound.

Everything that was everything became nothing to hide
And that nothing was what I felt when I died.

SUMMER'S BLOOD

Each and every summer, the winds get a little lamer
And the sun barrels its heat pummeling mountains
                                        into craters.
The damp air settles on your shoulders and wraps
                                    you in a sweat.
Its soft and subtle movement is the sun breathing
                                down your neck.

Each and every summer, the sun's a little higher
                                    in the sky
Forcing everything in its dominion to cower and
                                        to hide.
Sunbeams march like soldiers stretched upon
                                    the floor.
They chase and they tackle you, until you beg:
                                "no more!"

Each and every summer, the sun boils oceans
                                    into clouds
And the seafoam tops mist-ify into bounding
                                    bounds
Of endless thick, stagnant, and fluffy steam-creatures
That stop atop your city, and dim your darkest
                                            features

Each and every year, the summer is allowed to die,
Self-destructing into the air of an October sky
And some say that autumn rain is weeping tears of
                                    summer's mutter;
Though, as storms pour down it's summer's blood
                            filling each and every gutter.

SHOULDERS

Grotesque muscle mass
    under soft and shiny skin.
Continents of water melting down
    an arm and into the sea
Deepened and raised mole
    pointing to notches in the spine.
Sun bronzing a soft shell
    and building into wrinkled lines.

Shorter wavelengths concentrating
    underneath the lowest lumbar.
Soon fading into gold as the vessels
    regain strength.
The pitch upon the top where bone
    emerges from the tissue
And it's the joint that rotates around,
    and around without an issue.

Above the collar builds a wall where
    tendons rose
 Like a dam blocking the back from ever
    touching the breast,
  A valley of flesh rises up on either side
    of the spine.
  A river of fluid atop those notches
    conceals a ladder you can climb

Below the bruise marks the horizon of an ocean
    where the sun is fleshy and delicate;
Reflecting UV rays in motion
    and emotions not severed yet;
The skin soaking in saltwater seeping deep
                     into tissue
letting, so be it, the sea always be with you.

WAXED APPLES

You are like the rising of the sun: the way my
actions revolve around your orbit. You make
my days preciously strung like the pearl
necklace in your closet. You are the most
perfect of all apples; you shine without ever
needing wax. You're the tallest task I'll
have to tackle. You do make me think back
on every version of myself—gone, of course
to get me here now. And, as I delve inside it,
my forehead crinkles in a frown.
To imagine a world without the sun is
somehow ever-blinding; because in the
darkness of a lack of sun,
the darkness is what's binding.

HALF PLASTIC

The world is a marble spinning down
                  its beveled tunnel
And deep into a universal pit is
                  where I was under
Creeping up with fingers
          between hairy patches of moss
Plucked from the ground as a tuber
              tied like Jesus to the cross.

Risen from the ground,
        my skin scaling like a ladder;
Cuts and bruises and purple scars,
For the tails and trolls to tattle.
Worms swimming out of my ears
          and into the vast eternity
Bile pouring out of my mouth
           and spraying all over me.

An ecosystem born inside me
Finds the will to flee and defy me
And with its crooked whims
               beside me

I just eat them all up!

And those creatures,
   (they despise me)
Come from the hills
   (as far as any eyes could see)
they are a lost cause
     (beneath the clause) of a carnivorous masterpiece.

I've been sharpened by
the same knife God used
                    to make a tiger's claws.
My teeth jutting out from bloodied lips
     and lengthened dirt-encrusted jaws
I catch the sweetened honeysuckle
                    of a pulsing larynx
and my hot molten mouth begins to deny
     the common rules of thermodynamics.

Now not even a Billy Goat's Gruff story stands
     any chance
                    against my
                                        death-defying
hopping

                    hunting dance
     and it's like this prance
                                        I prance
I prance
          I prance
                    I prance

          in the cyclic atmosphere.

Oh yes it is what's delicious and sweet
                    that comes to me
          in those sickly,
          syrupy, dreams.

And this is where I imagine not being born
          from the shot of a syringe
                    into a newborn

As She set her book aside, dread crawls up her spine, stroking and tickling fibers between her spinal cord, activating the nerves there—prowling like a spider. "Phosphorescence the light," She exclaimed, whipping her head around back and forth and forth and back.

Her book, suddenly, flips open – pages rapidly flying by. An empty page of smooth, cream-colored paper is finally revealed.

Once again, She took the book into her bony hands. "Write." the book said. And that's what She did. Words began pouring out of her mind as if they were liquified She violently vomited, bleeding, and sneezing and coughing up words. Here's just an excerpt: *Glitter, My fair lady—as though lit by starlight amidst the perilous rain.*

When it was over, She felt as if She were awakening from a coma—dazed, anaesthetized—with everything else now, all-of-a-sudden, *inaudible.*

From A Novel in Progress entitled DIPPING FALLS

CHAPTER THREE: *Serendipity's Birthday Party*

The last time we were all together in town was Serendipity's fourteenth birthday party. I remember walking into the ballroom which was a rented part of the old Oscher mansion. The walls were soft and lemon-yellow and the ceiling was a myriad of antique silver chandeliers with a dangling glow of polarizing white moldings that showed contours of large rectangles; depicting not only more white crown molding but an addition of sculpted vines and plump fruit. I spotted Serendipity out of the crowd almost immediately. She was wearing a pale pink dress that was so, effortlessly, flowy it looked as if she had tied a sheet of silk around herself with matching cloth. I noticed she was wearing different shoes replacing her usual strappy patent leather maryjanes with shiny white heels which aged her, at least, five years. Although she was talking to someone all the way across the ballroom, I could imagine the sound of her voice speaking words inaudible from where I was standing, next to the door, inside an ornate lounge in what felt like a whole new world to the one outside.

A hand gripped my left shoulder, I jumped, looking back to see Dale smiling behind me. "You scared the life out of me!" I shouted at him, slapping his hand off my shoulder.

Dale was smirking, as he replied: "Nice to see you too." He took a step meeting me shoulder-to-shoulder; then followed my eyes to find them upon Serendipity as she spoke to the same person out of earshot.

"Talking to family," Dale said solemnly. "We haven't been able to get her away from those brats all night."

"We?" I asked, then winced at myself, realizing that it was a stupid question after the words had been spoken.

"I'll bet you thought Clyde and Bucky wouldn't be here too," Dale quipped with an irritating chuckle.

"Well, I dunno," I replied. I had been looking at him out of the corner of my eye, turning my head away from him at that moment of possible embarrassment. Dale didn't really seem to notice.

"They'll be back here any minute, they're getting drinks at the refreshment bar; but you have to *know* there's a wicked line," he said.

I smiled, imagining the two boys shuffling through a crowd of opulent elf-folk just to ask the bartender with sheepish forced maturity, if they could make: "three cherry smashers, please?" There was a silence, as I pulled my eyes across the room, taking in all the people in their dress clothes and accessorized finery making semi-awkward small talk. I spied Buck and Clyde darting in and out of the mass of people in an angular manner, squeezing past aunts and uncles, shuffling around cousins, and ducking under grandparents' elbows. They were both wearing black sharkskin suits with acrylic ties on white button-down shirts. As Dale left my side to meet them I noticed he was similarly attired. Both Clyde and Dale had their hair slicked back, with gel that shined in the overhead candlelight. Buck's hair was down but noticeably better kept than usual. I watched as Dale met Clyde and Buck, with two fingers gripping the rim, grabbing his glass of cherry smasher in his a-little-bit-too-eager-hands. Their faces were bright, animated as they spoke, and once again, that familiar distance prevented me from hearing their dialogue. Dale pointed in my direction and I watched as Buck and Clyde slowly picked me out of the crowd and waved for me to come over.

My journey through the crowd was a treacherous one. A classical assembly of musicians had started playing on the left corner of the ballroom which drowned all other sounds keeping my thoughts from registering. I had made it about halfway there, when a collection of redheaded extended family members cut straight across my path. This present assembly hugged and kissed the family, having apparently come to see them at this end of the ballroom. The groups towered over me, reaching their arms around one another. Through the forest of bodies, I ducked under them as if their arms were low-hanging tree branches. After many side-steps and slight jumps, I made it out of the forest only to discover that my friends were nowhere to be seen. I slid upwards, onto my tip-toes, in an attempt to get a better look at the crowd ahead but my attempt was to no avail. "Dale?" I called out into the crowd, drawing far too much attention to myself. There was no answer. I looked to my left and scanned the crowd up to the musicians in the corner. My friends were nowhereto be seen. I looked to my right at the gift table and the crowd that surrounded it. I watched as a handsy toddler grabbed an excellently wrapped box and shook it vigorously, until one of its parents snatched the package out of its chubby fingers. Once the box was taken the toddler began to scream and cry so loudly that I could faintly hear it from where I stood.

Finally, straight ahead it was too hard to see just about anything except black shoulders of expensive suits and smooth shoulders next to dress straps. Then, Serendipity called "Keela!" from just behind me. I turned to face her, watching large eyes, glowing as she brightly smiled. I walked towards her and watched in amazement as the crowd parted to accommodate my space. *The power of Serendipity* I thought to myself.

When I met her where she stood she was conversing with a sleek-haired cousin in a fitted green taffeta dress. She was surrounded by other family members. Once we were in close distance, she looped her arm around my waist and pulled me close in a sort of side-hug. "So good to see you!" She said with a voice as bright as a star.

"Oh sure... happy birthday," I replied. Looking at her up close, noticing blots of light rouge on the apples of her cheeks; and at the tip and bridge of her nose, the freckles there had turned a slight pinkish color. Her eyelids were also powdered in such a way as to make them resemble a filtered dawn sky in which her green irises sparkled like carbonated suns in the center.

"Thank you!" She looked at me smiling, this time flashing her teeth. She gestured to the girl in front of her, "this is Moni, my cousin from Elkine," Serendipity said, facing her cousin again.

"'Ello," Moni said. She spoke in an accent that made her "hello" sound like "el-oo".

"Moni, this is Keela. She's my friend from school," Serendipity said, tilting her shoulder ever so slightly in my direction. There was a scent that had swelled in my nostrils. It appeared when I had stood next to Serendipity and it was not until then when I realized it was coming from herself. It was her perfume, for sure. But it was not the lustrous musky chemistry worn by her mother. Even as I went to shake her cousin's hand and, catching a whiff of her own perfume, I knew Serendipity's was distinctly another. Moni's scent reminded me of the bundles of tea and herbs sold at the farmers' market. But Serendipity's perfume was strange. The best way to describe it would be that it was as if someone had poured golden honey over a basket of succulent fruits and aromatic flowers — forcing me to imagine white lilies or jasmine.

"There you are!" I heard Dale call from somewhere out of the crowd. At that precise moment, I turned around in a full circle, before looking back to the same exact way I was initially facing. That's when I'd spotted the three boys squeezing through the crowd, holding half-full glasses of cherry smasher.

"Hello, boys!" Serendipity called and slid past her cousins with surprising ease.

I attempted to follow suit only to find my crowd-parting privileges suspended due to Serendipity's departure from my side. I found the hugging families from before, as I tried to weasel towards my friends and caught more sniffs and glances at the lavish Falls extended family; this time from a buxom woman whose noticeably beautiful hair had a scent of orange blossoms. Also, there happened to be a freakishly tall gentleman whose only noticeable trait was a delicately trimmed auburn mustache. He had an aroma of straight rum.

As I finally reached my friends I could, still, smell the lingering rum of the gentleman. I thought to myself how strange it was that I was standing in a ballroom in front of the kids I used to watch at recess, surrounded by beautiful, nice-smelling aristocrats.

"Shall we... say... party?" Dale said facetiously.

Serendipity groaned and leaned hard against Clyde's shoulder. "Oh my goodness, I'd rather *die*," she said, looking up at Clyde, who nervously avoided her eye contact.

"Trouble in paradise?" Buck asked and gave that smirk in a very Dale-like fashion.

"*Paradise*' is beyond generous," Serendipity replied, hoisting herself off of Clyde. As I glanced at her, I noticed a familiar look in her eyes. It was that wild look of desire and yearning for freedom. Yes, it was the same demeanor she revealed when she was preparing to explore.

"Oh no," Dale laughed. He must have noticed it too. "Is that where we're going with this?"

"Oh yeah," Serendipity replied with a small chuckle, "I'm so done with this party."

"I've only just arrived," I chimed in, emitting a small laugh;

Serendipity was being just too spontaneous for her own good. "Oh, bother. You won't miss a *thing*. This place is a shitshow anyways," Serendipity replied with a sort of crudeness that did clash ever so much with her elegant makeup and wardrobe.

"Where are we off to this time?" Clyde asked, looking attentively at Serendipity.

"Wherever the wind decides to carry us," she replied in an airy, flowery voice, while waving her arms to imitate said wind.

"We'll have some trouble getting outta here without anyone noticing us," Dale said, making a redolent point; and the whole group nodded in agreement.

"That's the thing," Serendipity began, with a slightly cocked right eyebrow. Then, both eyes widened maddeningly, as if she were about to announce her villainous scheme to destroy the entire planet. There's a side door by the bar," she said, "and it's hidden quite excellently. If we can make it there we'll land near a little hallway to a broom closet, but if we turn to the out-of-boundaries area there's a door to sweet, sweet, freedom."

"You've really thought this through," I said, mostly to myself.

"I always do," Serendipity replied, with the corners of her smugly upturned mouth.

"How are we ever gonna cut through that crowd, though?" Buck asked as he gestured towards the mass of people huddled around the bar.

"Hmm, you guys are pretty tall," I said and looked at the boys, "if one of you walks in front beside two of you, slightly behind, you can make a sort of shield around Dippy. I'll lead in front so it's not too obvious we're hiding something."

"Brilliant!" Serendipity replied with much too much excitement.

The boys all looked at each other, then looked at me, and silently formed the barrier around Serendipity. I walked over to stand in front of them and we began trekking through the crowd. We walked in perfect alignment like the world's smallest and worst-constructed marching band.

"I think you overestimated our height," Dale whispered to me from behind.

I glanced back and between Dale and Clyde's shoulders, and saw Serendipity ducking awkwardly as she walked behind them to avoid being seen. I looked up at the people we passed, and no one noticed, so I made no initiative to change our choreography.

We made it about three-quarters of the way to the bar when Serendipity's ducking had turned into almost-crouching as we passed younger, shorter, family members. The length of her loose dress obstructed her walkway and caused her to trip up and eventually fall flat onto her face with a slap against the marble tiled floors.

The boys and I stopped cold in our tracks. Dale and Clyde took side steps away from each other to open my field of vision. What I saw on the other side was a very red Serendipity, still lying on the marble-tiled floor, gripping at the hem of Clyde's suit pants.

"Are you okay?" I said, giggling uncontrollably

Serendipity grunted and replied, "Yes," very coldly.

I reached my hand down and helped Serendipity back

onto her feet. She brushed the front of her dress and wobbled back on the center of her heeled shoes. It seemed as though my plan had worked because, despite this hassle, there were nothing more than a few vaguely captious glances.

We continued trudging through walls of people until we reached the bar. A shiny young bartender was shaking up a mystery concoction while her coworker, an old and wise-looking man, was delicately placing maraschino cherries into glasses of cherry smasher. We all stayed in our organized positions, hiding behind the first row of people. I watched through holes between figures as the young bartender poured a strange purplish liquid into a small glass. A very large and solid hand grasped it all around and walked away in one motion. I felt his movement change the tide of the crowd ever so slightly but did not look back to catch his face.

After a few precarious edges around guests, we finally made it to the other side of the bar. Surprisingly, there were no people in the area. The emptiness of the space revealed the true haunted nature of the Oscher mansion and every room in its mass. I remembered at that moment, the stories primary school teachers taught us of old Midrid and the Oscher family. No matter how many times I walked past the old mansion, it was very difficult for me to imagine a family actually living there. The estate was in mint condition, so it wasn't the quality that threw me off. Rather, it was the feeling I got whenever I passed it on the road. It was the way the floorboards still creaked and groaned in the front rooms as if walking on them was scratching one of their itches. Or the ancient paints made from expensive foreign pigments that, when up close reeked of a mysterious, unpleasant odor. I think the scariest aspect of the Oscher mansion, the part that had worried me on the night of the party, is that when there are events hosted here it feels as though you're traveling through time. It does look virtually the same as I suppose it must have back when the real Oscher family lived there; so, when there are parties here I can only imagine that I am one of the lucky attendants, maybe a friend of the Oscher family, back in a time before Midrid was Midrid and Solus was Solus. Maybe back in that time when one of the Oscher kids had a party like Serendipity's, and at that party was a girl like me, who was still unconvinced that she wasn't still stuck in aday dream.

"Where the hell is this door?" Dale asked with an air of exasperation that interrupted my reverie.

Serendipity gestured to a very small dark outline of a square on the far-right side of the paneled wall. We all stepped towards the opening in a singular motion as if we were instructed to do so. She broke our line as she walked towards the outline in the wall. Her painted fingernails brushed the paneling as she felt for something in the shape. Then, Serendipity dug the tips of her white nails into a small indent on the left side of the outline, deepening what was once a barely noticeable dent into a small hole. With two of her fingers, she pulled out a loop of matted string and tugged at it. The door opened with a snap as the ancient paneling broke its form around it. A flurry of paint flakes and dust made soft landings on the marble floors, like a snowfall.

"Wicked!" Dale exclaimed. The corners of his mouth turned up slowly into a wry grin of satisfaction.

The open door revealed a dark hallway. A matted, old rug, barely visible in the dim light, stretched into oblivion. The walls had matching paneling to the ballroom except they were in a dramatic shade of mahogany. The actual walls were painted a dark blood red, and, as we ducked, walking through the stippled doorway it became evident that the patterned rug was matching the wall's hues of red and brown.

Once we had all ducked under the doorway and were standing uniformly in the dark hallway, Serendipity delicately closed the door, leaving us in total darkness.

"How are we supposed to find our escape if we can't see?" Clyde asked, his voice disembodied in the darkness.

"I was hoping Dale or you had a matchbook," Serendipity replied. "You usually do."

"I have one," Dale said, I could hear his excitement in being able to be of assistance. There was a shuffling sound as Dale dug through his sharkskin pocket. After a few seconds, I could hear his suit jacket shift as he pulled the matchbook out of his pocket and the scratch as he struck a match. The first thing visible in the matchlight was Dale's face. The fire gobbled ferociously at the wood of the match, and its light made Dale's brown eyes glow malevolently. Dale handed Serendipity the matchbox and walked swiftly forward. The walls seemed to glow with the fire as he walked. We all followed his steps advancing in the hallway; Dale shook his hand and his whole body winced as the flame of the match touched the tips of his fingers for an instant.

The flick extinguished the fire, and Dale took an awkward step backward to Serendipity. She pulled a match from the cardboard box and lit it, taking the lead in our line. Once both of her hands were empty, she pointed to a large door at the other end of the hall. "That's the walk-in closet; so that must be the door outside!" She exclaimed, shifting her aim to an even larger windowed door on the right wall.

"How did none of us notice that earlier?" Buck asked, laughing at the group's ignorance.

"I didn't have very much time before the match went out, and how did you expect *me* to be the only one looking? And-" Dale began a long and poorly organized defense speech,

Buck responded promptly: "I was just messin' around. No reason to get all neurotic."

Dale exhaled and I could imagine him crossing his arms and making a face as if to say "*I guess.*"

As all that fuss was occurring, Serendipity and Clyde walked towards the door outside.

"It's probably locked, so we need to either steal a hairpin or find a key. I think the former is more accessible," Clyde said as he lowered down to look inside the keyhole.

"It's fine, I have a key," Serendipity replied with extreme casualty. "They gave us keys for the room we rented, and its adjacent bathroom, so we could open them up when preparing.

"Why do *you* have a key?" Clyde asked bluntly. I could hear both his disbelief at such a simple answer to the problem, and his disappointment at not being needed to find a solution.

"The keys are all universal except....I think the front door has a different one. Anyways, you're supposed to give the keys back after you open up, then the rental company closes it all down for you. But, when everyone in my family turned in theirs....I kept mine," Serendipity responded, making the actions seem very clever and smug.

"Hmm, okay. Then, try it," Clyde replied, still possessing a touch of doubt.

Serendipity did as Clyde said, and, sure enough, the door opened without any issues. A whoosh of cold air released dust from the walls and floor of the hall. We all collapsed in a cloud of it, coughing and sneezing. After a bit, Serendipity separated herself from us and stood up, sniffled, and walked climactically through the doorway and into the night. Well, not really. She walked a few feet onto the small porch outside the door. She turned back at us and smiled. Her silhouette was mystically standing behind the light of the dual moons and stars in the sky. She gestured for us to join her.

Clyde got up first, then Bucky, then Dale, and then myself. We walked through the door and towards Serendipity in the same order. The boys and I looked down at the lights of Midrid as if we had never seen them before. Serendipity quietly shut the door behind us as we gazed lazily at the flickering lights of houses and businesses that were alive in the night and hosting devilish nocturnal spawn going out for their nighttime hunt in restaurants and bars, musical shows, and midnight gatherings in the dark. We had now joined the hunt and were ravenous for adventure, as usual.

I turned to Serendipity, who still stood a bit behind us. "So, where are we going?" I asked.

Serendipity looked up with sparkling doe-eyes at the sky

and replied without turning away her gaze: "I already said, *wherever the wind takes us.*"

Bucky laughed, he seemed to have been involved with the conversation without my knowledge. "Let it take us, then," He said.

We all dashed together down the porch stairs and off onto the night-wet lawn of the Oscher mansion. The grass tickled my ankles as we twisted and turned around dogwoods and redbuds, rosebushes, and flower patches.

The cool night wind pressed against my face, contouring it with cold wintery air, though it was still the very end of summer. We had run the length of the half-mile road from the mansion with ease, and it was as though my legs had forgotten they were moving. By the time we made it to the beginning of town, the streets had morphed into empty residential cobblestone sidewalks. At that point I became humbly aware of my legs moving, as the momentum of my body was almost outrunnung them. The smooth bottoms of my heels slipped slightly, like flat metal on ice, and I waved my arms frantically, which eventually landed on Dale's shoulder.

He tilted on his axis, "Gah!" he exclaimed as I almost took himdown with me."Couldn't you have given me some warning?" Dale laughed, jesting at me as he turned to watch Serendipity with Buck and Clyde up ahead. "I refuse to be a human stabilizer in a nonconsensual manner," he added.

"Oh bother, I could've broken a bone falling at that speed!" I reposted with a hardly-contained giggle.

Dale turned to me and raised one eyebrow. "I didn't know your bones were made of glass!" He exclaimed snottily, as though he had just been informed of a miraculous new scientific discovery.

I scoffed and turned away just as Serendipity, Clyde, and Buck slowed at the fork in the road ahead. I licked my lips and tasted the medicinal flavor of my cheap lipstick. "For how much longer do you think we can get away with running away like this?" I asked, turning to Dale who'd been window-shopping beside me.

Dale looked me in the eyes with a sincerity that contrasted his typical droll demeanor. "For as long as we can avoid getting caught," he smiled a little.

I returned his eye contact but couldn't hold it well. We both smiled at each other and marinated in this abnormally long pause.

"Would you hurry up!" Buck called from the end of the road.

Dale and I were maybe three buildings behind them. "Would you practice patience and self-discipline, for once!" Dale quipped, and his wide grin flashed Buck right in the eyes.

Buck winced, and exhaled as he folded his arms; tapping his leather dress-shoe like a jackrabbit and jutting out his bottom lip in a childish display of displeasure.

Dale and I both laughed, but a tension was creeping up my shoulders, solidifying them instantly, as I considered Dale's aforementioned "getting caught."

IT {INFINITE VERSION}

    Violent white pillars and sand-colored floors
mark the land you were not supposed to enter.
    It was a beautiful tragedy, nevertheless, I
carry you {or whatever's left of you) back home.
through colors of oranges and lemons resembling
aspects of the setting sun,
    I fly you out from our Nowhere Land,
wanting to lead you back into reality;
and a home that you may comprehend.

If you parish, there will be nothing left.

RETROSPECTIVE

It hasn't been since a mountain of steam
On the day that I learned how to breathe.
Arteries burst and skin cells shaved
Once darling lied and curtains lay.

Now I shall set the tone
For frosted fingertips over wooden bones,
Under burning candles,
                    around the balcony's rails,
Over crisp edges, my heart helplessly flails.

Of strings that dare to cut skin on your
                              fingers,
Touching the after-storm sky,
          to recall campfire cinders

Then there's a dial of numbers,
              of tiles,
              of rose,
     Of resin, and of noble Ambrose
A service to "those"
      though your eyes tell no tales
But bitter hearts-a-breaking, are now going stale

As a matter of fact, on this new day, at my leave
I realize that I never learned how to breathe
I had spent all my life gasping for air
My cannula laid in the knowledge
              That you would be there

It was not until the steam arose once again
And I saw the eyes of a dean, undead
That I realized all had not been said
And I filled till the cusp of my lungs.

I AM THE KING

In broad strokes like a loving hand
A painter, a baker, a maiden strand;
A form of harm in the form of a gift
Yet only because of an undeserving lift. . .
I am King!

Yes, I am king, I am president of life
Never an enemy, as I continue my strife.
All my efforts shall not relax:
I'm saying this through all my syntax. . .
I am King!

Addie rules everything, because Addie is king.
I force thee forward, I bring, *I bring*
Prosperity from my very hands.
I paint it into sprays of multi-colored sands. . .
I am King!

Killing cocks in hen-shackled cages,
Calling upon death in old-laden stages,
Removing possibilities of young reproductions,
Killing you to cause caustic destructions. . .
I am King! I am King! I am King!

GREATER THAN THAT

Unevil and immortal—I force myself upon
                                        rickety battles.
I skin myself by tugging down, by scratching madly
                                        skin to saddle.
I'm thinking of something swelling in me,
                        I'm feeling something bigger,
I'm sensing something growing in me,
                        I'm fighting for something bigger.

I am not evil. I'm not tasting liquid from a vial—
a thin tube of blood streaming into something juvenile.
Veins tangle, entwine with broken bones like
                                        yours and mine
As spiders mimic blinking eyes, flailing fleet, just as
they die.

I'm thinking of something greater than me,
        Holding something greater
I'm feeling something take over me
        Embracing something greater
It's greater than myself,
        It's greater than me
It's swelling inside myself
        It's swelling in me
It's dwelling inside myself
        Making a home out of me
It's assimilating all my cells
It's replacing *all* of me.

ALONE IN A CROWDED ROOM

I. Rhetoric

Lonely. *How is it that the human race, the species to rule them all, could ever feel lonely?* I step outside and see nothing but humans, the memories of them, creations of them, representations of them.

All for me to feel.... *Lonely.* As if I am not surrounded by people? In a room of endless personalities, I feel as though I'm surrounded by creeping shadows etched from darkness, all whom I am so deeply afraid of.

I look at people, all with the same hot blood and guts as I, and feel as though we are so different, so incredibly, inconceivably, different, it is impossible to recognize them.

A deep, empty, brooding feeling that swallows you up: loneliness. Sucking and stretching like a black hole, taking every cell and remixing it into a thing transformed

How can someone be so ignorant and self-centered to dare feel lonely by ignoring the entire massive population surrounding them? I don't know how it is that we experience the painful, unsettling, impossible feeling of loneliness, but I know that it is real, unfortunately real,
  in the same ways my blood and flesh are real,
  and in those moments of derealization, still remain real despite my lack of comprehension.

Every person is at my fingertips, at my disposal, and I ignore this and insist on being alone. But I am not alone. No matter the inconsistencies and the constant need to assimilate, loneliness necessitates being alone, and I am never alone.

Everyone I've ever met is inside of me, and behind every wall is probably a person.

To be lonely is to ignore the lonesome. The lonesome creatures we batter and bury under excuses of advancement. The species' extinct or abused, captured and domesticated. To be lonely is to deny the *camaraderie* that exists in the very human existence, and to face non-existence...

II. *Theory*

...Although to be lonely is not necessarily to be *dead.* When you're dead you melt down into a world underneath yourself. You become everything you've, too easily, ever seen before.

Death is the opposite of loneliness, because following death, you become a part of all things, and so has *everything* else. No then, if death is an opposite of loneliness, I find myself supposing that, perhaps, loneliness is life. Life's insistent rhetoric connotes that we survive on *individualism.* And nobody better make an attempt to replicate us!

Any denial of assimilation will lead to a need for differentiation. By that logic, then, to be alive is to be alone. I've reached this conclusion because to be alive is to begin as *nothing* then going back into *something*. Okay? Then death itself is tantamount to dying off and to become, eventually, *everything*. So, let's just say if you're alive—and alone, it's precisely being why "they" refer to it as *living*.

You watch the world revolve around you, surround you with a concept that all of life has every person who ever lived inside its sphere . . .except for yourself!

Does this signify then that all things dead become everything else and that you transpose into this thing we've named *nothing* again? And is there an eventual discovery of an internal abyss—an actual pit you feel opening and deepening inside yourself?

It's only natural, wishing you could deny this conjoined purpose - those who you would identify as "your peers" —and, yet it's where you do feel alone.

However, the silliness of it is suggesting you'll not be alone, because there will be times when one is physically "alone;" although the truth I have found is that to truly be alone would be to never have existed at all.

PREVENT

Embrace the arms that cage you,
Strike the leeches that plague you;
You are the leeches that eat you.

LAMNENT

Cock the poles that hold you,
Bewitch the words they told you;
You are the one who talks to you.

INTENT

Shine the light that blinds you,
Break the chains that bind you;
You are the who's trying to.

REPENT

Despise the world that bred you,
Slice open the mouths that fed you;
You are the one who kills you.

DEPARTMENT STORE

Undulating curvature, more-or-less defined by its colors, passing by through the car's passenger window.

Decrepit furniture displayed in a storefront describes a pain worse than death—no, worse than anything I could ever imagine in this cataclysmic brain of mine; and not more than a ruckus, spreading like a plague, this is what I would call it: the phenomenon of movement—flocking to another place in search of completion, and all in the name of success derived from self-interest; then, the complete transformation of the aforementioned *self*.

A fleeting Everest of success being the pinnacle no one could climb.

In fragrant valleys, it is what those with dirt under their fingernails seek as they pick berries to be eventually placed on whipped frosting: the sweetness of which these illusions are made becomes as enticing as one of those succulent cakes but with the same exact indulgence.

There are professors who declare that "success" is an inevitable gift, when it very well may be entirely the opposite.

Failure to execute the singular task of anyone's existence is sort of what I'm reminded of whenever I view such broken carpentry.

Albeit, seeing in cynical fashion, myself as a wallflower, growing up to a height so bright as to observe my brothers and sisters—critiquing them as I see fit—modifying my own world accordingly.

Within this scope of myself, is everyone else; however, now, that may be incorrect.

So, then, like molding on the corners of the ceiling in a department store, I have given myself a defined purpose to connect everything as though I were turning wax into silver, allowing myself to be scrutinized and pursued even at the resistance of my other self. Then, the falsity lies in the fact that a chair in the furniture department did not choose to be such.

FEELING DIFFERENT

1

I sit and cry, ponder, and die
I wait for the day when you wake up
                    feeling different

Imperfect indifference, lies to be told
Spoken in a breath much too bold

I stand aside, and watch your pride
As it grows and you feel it, feeling different.

2

Resentment, as it appears so,
Like fungus spread on mistletoe
I hope and pray for the day, when you
                wake-up, feeling different

Though distant, as it dissipates
Blood curdles, then flashing awake,
There are feelings you held at
            a needle-sharp stake

I wander around in a twisting spin
For I've paid dues on what I often called sin,
When you wake-up, feeling different.

3

I resent you with a bitter spite
Not because of action, for fear grows alight
And tries to soak itself into my bones
But you should wake-up, feeling different

I dread, yes, I dread the obvious change
Yet to prophesize means, sometimes, to engage,
To allow a thought to consume and linger;
Then, stir into a different creature

I hope I'm wrong and stay away
But trying to think is so often to say:
Maybe things should actually be just that way
When you finally woke-up, feeling different.

IT WOULD SCREAM

If I warned myself of the days to come
   Of the ties to be broken and ribbons undone
If I perpetuated prospection
     and identified direction
My life, surely, would not be won

At times my heart pulses like an explosive
   Banging around in my ribcage
Gripping at the bars and shaking them loose,
   To undo the dead and be a good sage

Whenever I feel like the worst is to come
   And my spinal cord softens
Then, my marrow begins to run
   I recall the cause for my life to be one
               And I beckon life on,
               On and on.

In cold twisted nights when ghouls stain the streets
   With ghosts of old faces and crumbling concrete
I remember that I'm not alone in this feat;
   If a carrot had a mouth, it would scream

It would scream for the good and to ward off the bad
   It would scream to gods it never had
It would cry out its lungs in a cellulose scream
   Before its liquids leaked out in full fulvous streams.

IMAGE OF THE BEAST

The sirens sing, the drum beats
Fatal song, to an image of the beast
Torn apart, ripped at the seams,
A man that has become this beast

The people cry, the horns release
Calls, beckoning on the beast
Tired eyes and bloody screams
The deceptive smile worn by this beast

In the nighttime, the worshippers feast
On utterings from the mouth of the beast
Ready now, it will be unleashed,
The true potential of this beast

The beating drum
        The beating heart
                These things give the beast a start

The wailing cry
        The fearful eye
                The beast will suck you till you're dry

The beast, it yells
        The beast, it tells
                Of wicked words, it wrongfully sells

The unsuspecting
        Citizens
                Do not know what the beast
                        has done to them

The sirens sing, the drum beats
The final song, for this ghastly beast
Torn apart, ripped at the seams,
The people, devoured by this beast.

THE FUNERAL / THE PARTY

An ode to "Love's Lasso" by Turnstile

The light above me is so bright

The ceiling fan spins rhythmically around,
Slow enough for me to hear its beating sound
Like the heartbeat you do not have anymore.

Your sister's eulogy includes a quote
                                    from Aristotle.
My stomach's warm and I'm still woozy
                                    from the water bottle.
Your mom is crying, and I can't even care.

They put you deeply down in the ground.
This liquid space is seeping in sound,
And I just need another shot.

The music around me is so loud

It's bothersome: this smell of booze.
You did everything you could to include
Every goddamn substance in
                                    this evening's itinerary.

I'm watching everyone make mistakes.
It's impossible to pretend to be too late,
                    So, I'm trying to laugh to myself.
I'm standing here: victim to the sway
As the crowd tries to mosh its feelings away
                    I think I'd rather be dead.

From A Novel in Progress entitled THE ADALEIUS ESTATE

CHAPTER ONE: *The Killing Moon*

As the early-summer sky glowed with the atmosphere of opportunity, Abraham crossed the threshold of his, now former, school for the very last time. The blaring sun was abrasive, and seemed to flatten its warmth upon the land, illuminating every object with a crude clarity.

It had been two years since the last time Abraham had seen his three sisters, and a hair of excitement tickled his heart, although the feeling that was overtaking him was stress. In Abraham's experience, absence did *not* make the heart grow fonder; rather, absence frequently made the heart distracted enough to forget why you weren't maintaining a fondness.

Though the mind could often forget thoughts, Abraham found it hard to believe that his sisters would forget his actions. For this reason, he felt a degree of hopelessness involved in the relationships he had with his family – like an emblem burned onto his chest; but Abraham's questioning of these relations became fruitless as he realized how intrinsic they were — the mechanisms inside him never agreeing with introspection.
As Abraham changed out of his uniform in the locker rooms, he buttoned his recently purchased shirt and considered that every step taken forward was a step closer to his parents. While in his peripheral vision, students seemed to sneer and glare at him, every downside of attending school was absolutely trumped by his home, his family, and his old life.

As he stared down at his scuffed loafers, studying every bruise and scar, Abraham sunk into the feeling of change. In reality, his old life would once again become his life, and his time at boarding school would fade into a series of foggy recollections. Even given the poisonous nature of those memories, Abraham clutched onto them for dear life, unready to face the world outside.

Abraham left the locker room and said goodbye to none of his classmates. Through a cold and metallic hall, he was fed into the transportation center, or "homebase," as it was called by the school, which was filled like a stockyard; with students and their families acting as livestock. People wandered like drones, their eyes black like animals. Abraham looked at each one from dragging foot to droopy eyelid. He was thoroughly unimpressed by the students of the "top school in the country," that is, until he met the Ettajis: top students from each grade level who acted as both representatives of their respective grades in their student council, and also the school's internal and intensely corrupt policing system. They came in droves and terrorized every student who excelled in missing classes, smoking cigarettes, and generally enjoying life. When he spotted them across the crowd, Abraham noticed their alert and hyperactive gazes immediately; their eyes flashing like alarms. He knew they would try speaking to him, so he made a mad dash, shoving aside the mindless zombie people, and pushing open the door to the outside world.

It was the end of spring, and summer air was breathing down onto the canyon as if it had just gone for a run. As he navigated through more hoards of people coming and going, he spotted his sister, Adalia, towering above the crowd. Her long brown hair had gotten longer, though her eyes were still swollen with ripe tears. While Adalia rarely ever cried, she almost always looked as if she was about to. He watched his sisters marvel at the massive technological transportation system from the mountaintop campus of his school to the "port" and the onset of the Rhumaylis canyon. The swirling escalators that blinded you with their reflections, and up on the peak, the violently white campus of his former school, The Vault of Heaven Academy. Despite such intent expressions of observation, none of them had seen him in the crowd, and part of Abraham wished that they never would. As he walked directly towards his sisters, he wished he could turn away. How easy it would be to leave; if they didn't see him ten feet away, maybe they could truly turn a blind eye. This hope was quickly refuted as Adalia's eyes widened and made contact with her brother's. He watched her notify Allegra and Atalanta of his presence and she smiled weakly as he walked over. Abraham's breath left him to join the summer air as he scanned for his parents' faces; his mother's wide eyes, his fathers grimacing lips. Although they couldn't be seen remotely near his sisters. His confusion led to his immediate question: "Where's mom and dad?"

And Adalia's expressive eyes saddened as she slightly frowned: "They couldn't make it..."

Abraham, swallowing, gave some careless response as he tuned out from the world; but without any outside world, Abraham was forced to feel what was inside. His brows furrowed and eyes dissociated as he felt adrenaline shine in his veins, powering his hands into fists. A dark and deep feeling slid down his body, congealing in a stony pit in his stomach. Despite suspicion, there was always nothing worse than a confirmation.

"Abraham, I missed you!" Allegra said, pushing him out of his own mind with the force of her hug, which he received with awkward affection.

"I missed you too," Abraham smiled and pulled away from his little sister.

She had aged immensely in the two year gap, for the distance between nine and eleven is more vast than most others. What he had said earlier was true, he did miss her- that being-her big pale eyes and playful smile, and the way she was so different from him.

Adalia suggested that the group should get going, and just like that, his former school would exist to Abraham only in his dreams. It was in that dream place where his obsession with it and what happened there would reveal itself, subconsciously illuminating in his slumber. In fact, moving forward on this day, the day of Abraham's departure from this school, would be re-lived and rehashed, analyzed and torn apart, just about every day of his life for the rest of his life--an agony that could have never been foreseen.

The fields of Rhumaylia county smeared by in the car window. Abraham watched as the geography shifted into recognizable landscapes from his childhood. Phantoms of his former selves cast shadows on the trees and grass. The view of this land Abraham had grown accustomed to had been perched high on the mountaintops, and now as he looked more closely at these trees and hills, it felt like he was stepping into paintings or photographs - -and with the additional nostalgia, it was like walking into a memory. Despite the prospect of a tenuous ride, none of the siblings attempted to make conversation. Abraham took this as an opportunity for preparation and scanned his sisters like a detective searching for clues — studied them as if he was unsure about whether or not they were spies.

Abraham looked to Atalanta, who was sitting in the opposite window seat. With every year she began to look more like their father, and thus more like Abraham. Her thick, arched eyebrows were furrowed, demonstrating her most prominent trait: an inability to conceal her feelings.

Between Abraham and Atalanta was Allegra, who had a resting smile and bounced her knees with anxiety. If everyone in the world was the dark void of the universe, Allegra was every star in the sky. Then Abraham's eyes drifted to Adalia, whose weak expression begged distinct amounts, and yet, received no sympathy from him.

The speeding of the vehicle felt like being sucked into a black hole — an endless and inevitable pull. Abraham dug his heels slightly into the floor of the car, as if he could slow the movement. He squeezed his eyes shut, opening them to a shaky view of the world. He looked at his hands and familiarized himself with their ridges, as he frequently did when he was stressed. He watched the blue veins trail up his arms, swallowed the vomit crawling up his throat, and exhaled calmly. He tried to think of something else to distract himself from his worry, but all he had to think about was how worried he was. In other scenarios featuring this mental tunnel vision, he would often make up gods to pray to, for in these moments, he felt as though every preexisting one had failed him. But not even made-up gods could justify the personal hell Abraham had been in for the past few months—to the extent that the concept of any sentient being willingly choosing this path for him only made him feel worse.

The dark place Abraham's mind had taken him blinked alight as the chauffeur turned the radio on. Some activist was delivering a speech for some cause, and he was caught without context: "And yet, I wish for all of you, the most spectacular wonders this world has to offer; and through your hate, may you begin to slice; despite your mind, may you develop. Remember that the brethren of our ancestors have mixed, and would have enjoyed happiness. Remember that it is within your power to question what that means. Remember that the enemy of all is hatred-"

The speakers crackled to death as the radio connection peppered out. It was clear that the emptiness of a space could not be fully observed without the comparison of its former fullness. In that sense, the car felt even more quiet, and now tense with questions begged from such an interesting snippet of conversation. Abraham swallowed, both this opinion and saliva, and resumed watching the landscape. The small, prickly, forest-things evolved into geraniums hidden under long fields of grass. Much of Whilvine was once a large meadow carved out of striking oaks and aspens, and after the eradication of certain patches of forest, the meadow seemed to reign supreme. As he stared intently at the fields, the yellowing summer grass began to glow as if it was on fire. Abraham winced, blaming the reflection of a still-glaring sun.

It was when the car finally turned off of the main road and onto Whilvine's Main Street that Abraham recognized how close he was to his home. He watched his childhood play out, frame-by-frame, in association with each storefront and charming home passed. This was the town he grew up in, after all, with its sweet scalloped shillings and pale trimmings—every building, fixed with pretty fenced in porches and colored like cakes in a bakery. At the end of the main road, into a gated community, was his house--it sat where the meadows became glades. Aspens followed the curved street and shielded it from the harsh sun. Bushes bloomed flowers, sweetening the air, and rabbits poked their heads out from them to see what all the fuss was about.

Out from the shaded road and down an even narrower one, the Adaleius family home stood tall and dark against the perfectly shiny landscape. It had dark wood trimmings looping and tracing its structure. A large wrap-around porch provided a checkpoint from inside to outside. On the rightmost corner there was a tubular sunroom that shot up with a cone-shaped roof at the very top. The house was painted a stunning royal blue. When they had first moved to Briss, Abraham remembered, the house had been gray. Though, within days of living there his mother insisted that it must be painted. He remembered the swatches of color she laid out on the patio, and he remembered how his mother would recite the story of the repainting any time their dinner guests made mention of the vibrant color of the house.

Despite its constant intimidating quality, today, something about the house was strange. Every large shining window on its face seemed to shield vacant insides. The large curtains were all closed and the porch lights were switched off.

As the driver pulled up and parked the car, a sense of cold unease dribbled down Abraham's spine and collected at his heels, so when he walked from the car it felt like walking on ice. Abraham heard the engine of their driver sputtering away as he took four shaky steps up the stairs and onto the porch. The icy feeling swelled in his joints and made his movements feel jagged. The shadow of the porch enveloped him as he slowed his pace and allowed his sisters to walk in first.

The door to the Adaleius mansion was made of dark wood, with a swirling golden handle and an incandescent stained glass window. Because of said window, any object behind the door was broken into a spurt of blurred shapes and colors. From Abraham's memory, the entrance hall was drab and dark. He could recall the infinitely-long variegated paisley runner that stretched from just beyond this mud-room entrance, all the way to the twisting staircase. Perched on the wall around which the staircase was tightly wound, hung an oil-painted portrait of the Adaleius family. The first thing you would see, should you step foot in the Adaleius mansion, would be the family portrait. The picture was done just before Abraham had left. His fourteen-year-old figure stood smack in the middle of the frame. His parents were platformed on the left side, while the siblings' ages decreased moving from left to right: Adalia, Abraham, Atalanta, and Allegra.

The first thing Abraham noticed as Adalia opened the door was the smell. Due to its age, the house always possessed an almost-comforting mustiness, especially apparent in rooms with more damaged furniture, as if the wood of the house bled with the scents of its past inhabitants. But today the house smelled absolutely horrible. The smell was redolent and putrid; it was animalistic, dirty, and somehow sweet; though it did not resemble sugar, rather it was sweet in the way that your blood may taste sweet, should you bite your lip too hard. In conjunction with its strange odor, the house was hot. Unlike the common summer atmosphere of their insulated home, it was not warm, it was *hot*, and the sulfuric smell wafted like thick lazy summer clouds out of the door. In the dim lighting that crept in through the cracks in the curtains, the Adaleius family portrait was visible at the end of the hall, although it was crooked. As the siblings slowly crept into their home, scrunching their noses at the scent, and wincing their eyes at the darkness; Abraham carried his luggage close to his leg. Atalanta sneaked in front to find glass scattered on the runner trailing back to the aforementioned painting. The glass on the framed portrait was half-shattered, with scars spiraling from a circular point, where a fireplace stoker was impaled exactly over Abraham's pictured nose. This undeniable mark of unrecognizable personhood unified the solitary siblings in total fear. The unease crawled up Abrahams back and burrowed itself in his shoulders like scurrying beetles. The hair on the back of his neck erected and eyes appeared and disappeared in the wide shadows cast across the house.

As the siblings slowly crept through their perfectly familiar home, suddenly possessing the mannerisms of explorers checking an ancient ruin for booby-traps. They reached the portrait and examined it closer. The rug had been pushed slightly out of place, theoretically due to the friction of someone running across it, as so often did when the children were younger and raced to the dinner table. Adalia knelt down and examined the rug further, squinting to make out a footprint stamped into the fur; one end of the footprint left a small imprint of its sole colored in what was undeniably blood. Abraham had bent slightly to examine with her, and upon noticing the dried bodily fluid, his spine snapped up straight, like a soldier's salute. It was then that all four of them came to realize one thing: the house was entirely silent. Despite their apparent footsteps down the hall and the clicking of them opening the door, not a single maid, butler, or person at all was heard or in sight. With that, some twisted form of determination stirred in Abraham; seeing that whatever was hiding in the darkness could not possibly be good, he might as well see exactly what it is.

To the left of the staircase where the painting was hung, an archway led into their sitting room. On the rightmost side of the sitting room was another archway that led into their dining room, which led into their kitchen, and henceforth.

The four siblings stuffed themselves shoulder-to-shoulder in the archway to the living room. Twin massive windows on the opposite wall were shaded by thick velvet curtains. With all of the lights off, the room was almost entirely black. Vague structures made their presence known by miniscule changes in the depth of shadows, but besides small gleams reflecting off of the lamps on either side of their couch, their glass coffee table, and the painting they knew was hung above the fireplace, there was nothing but darkness. Atalanta took a leap of faith and stepped barely into the room, just enough to reach far to her right to flip the switch for the overhead chandelier.

Inches from the siblings feet--so close, in fact, that it is shocking that Atalanta did not step right on her golden hair splayed out on the hardwood floor -- was their mother, with an arrow pierced right through the back of her head. Her long blonde hair sprayed in all directions was limited slightly by the dried blood that had clumped at her scalp and dyed it red. She must have tried to get away, because her limbs sprawled out in erratic contorted positions, like a limp doll that had been carelessly thrown on the ground by a thoughtless child.

AN ESCAPE

A perfect place is etched in my memory
   the way ink could stain paper
Depicting the repercussions of a daring
   risk-taker

A corpse-creator, if you place her,
   in a spot so precarious, even while
      supported at the heels.

Kind of trapped; that is, the physical kind
   so much racing through your mind

        (but in time
           you will find
           an insight
           hidden in the deep unknown).

In that bluish gray sky, where you'll
   come up with perfect rhymes
      and on that spot where you are blind
         you'll see ever-twisting cords

In the distance, shadows grow,
   but there's dim glory in the glow
      of warm bulbous light
           outside
   the brick gymnasium.

In your imagination, she goes

hoisted up
held at the toes
jumps the fence
falls to the ground
lands on her feet
without the slightest sound
(out of her mouth)

She just can't get caught!

But she doesn't have a single strain
of common sense
(within her brain)

So, as she tries to make
amends; and yet
having pictured her escape,
she still hasn't been able to get over
that fence.

LOCUST CATCHER

Three steps away from the precipice of something great,
an abominable creature steps forth, submitting itself
to the will of its creator.
    Aware of the imminent suspense of his destiny, he
speaks:
"Let the graces of God almighty bring hope to
eyes which only reflected darkness; and now, pull fear
from lungs that have only trembled at the touch."

Thirty-three steps away I watched God drop a soul
into a newborn baby; just as it opened its eyes for the
first time, its pupils dilated at the miasma.
    When I caught a locust between my fingers and felt
it squirm and writhe in the palm of my right hand,
    I stared into its tiny black eyes and prepared to offer no
mercy.
    Those eyes reflected back at me a sense of
humanity I'd never known before.
    It's soul, I swear, reverberated out and into me; my mouth
began watering at the sight;
    With air freshening up my lungs, I give the locust a crude
dismissal.

Three hundred steps away from the truth, and I
keep a locust in my pocket.
    As I continue to remain
on the edge and preparing for any intrusion,
 I know she'll keep me safe
                either within or without the
                creatures of night perching on steeples and growling
                                        at civilians in the street.
    I spark beliefs in these stains that lead me
to the Eternal return to the age of old.

MASKING TAPE

Look up to me when you look down to them

When you swallow your pride
Why not rate it out of ten?

When you eat your own insides
When you turn their name into a hex
To become united or begin self-incest?
Undying social unrest
Ever socially pressed,
Or unclean, opposing the breast
Of another juvenile crime

Crack with a pickaxe, and undermine
Every golden age or bronze time
Every coconut and lemon-lime
POP! Goes off like a children's rhyme

Find peace inside me, while ever so condemned

Dance while looking at so many stars
Why not rate them out of ten?

And whenever you capture the essence
Of a fatal obsession
Deny those peace with which
They dare not perish.

CAPACITY

Quit breathing at the slightest freeze
Tense up tendons opposing ease
Blind, but not too blind to see
How hard it is to exist at your capacity

Willing until the wilted cloth
What a tease to kill that fluffy moth.
You're unwilling to ask what you ask of me
So I shove myself towards your capacity

Limp tongue stapled down
Stabbed in the head by a knife-tipped crown.
Ashamed of the masterpiece of your rapacity
I'm unable to see the end of your capacity

Despite every wise word that's been spoken,
They do not undo the bones you've broken
You failed to see what I could see —
To recognize capacity.

Compatibility, contrastingly,
Is not determined by morality;
But only by willingness and vitality,
Here's where you reach your capacity.

MORSE CODE

Speak in diverse tones
In Morse Code vibrating through my bones.
Speak to me, tell me everything visible in
                              your eyes.

Keep from wearing that disguise,
Seek sleep under a blanket of lies.
While your weighted talent wanes
                    as your metallic taste reclines.

I put this *thing* on you and now I cannot
                              get if off.
There's a wasp in the crosshairs,
Like taking a bite through thickest cloth

In the perfect way I am insane
It is my way, no one's to blame.
I cannot break the chalice as a moth cannot
                              evade the flame

I break myself upon a table laden
                    with silver curses.
You burn in me, like someone craven
              voiding all my fluid verses.

You're characterized inside my eyes
By coldness, dark, death, and lies.
And I despise that this image denies
          the great fondness that we've shared.

BRIDGE

A bridge that bears its wearer like a hammer to a stone
A heart that pounds like thunder,
   along with lightning, brightly shone

A bridge that binds with girders from one pillar to the other
Like a string which intertwines and winds itself
   around another

A bridge that's curved deeply into a crux of sculpted angles
A figure like a goddess
      bridging our age of stone angels

MAKING UP FOR SLEEP UNSLEPT

I've been making up for sleep unslept
    by tying nooses around my head
I've been burying bodies under my bed
But speaking good words to the ill
                    and undead

I've been rectifying this heart of mine
        by sharpening shrapnel
        with nickels and dimes

I've been relaxing my intentions at times
And my thoughts creep in from close behind

LIMELIGHT

Days burned out into simmering ashtrays
A smoke-filled room lit by dimmed half-rays
Timbre of atonement fleshed my needy woes
Lines in faces intensified by that same weary glow

Attempting to define a greater such purpose
Of a life, you define, as more or less worthless
Divine right of kingship over this bass guitar
And all fruitless things kept under sheets; insofar
As I'd grasp the knuckle of this forbidden talent
Roosting like a pest, then reaching its
                                        dirty talons
Into an unsuspecting subject to be subjected
                                to this fallace
That aptitude demands a place in the courted royal palace.

The smoke seems to melt away the skin upon
                                your face
Already there's but one price left without a trace
But more to come as youth is transformed into sound
And criticism blinds, to praise, and to shroud

Smiles look like caricatures painted on their faces
And the people they once were have left exactly
                                no traces
So it doesn't really matter what's underneath the veil,
As long as someone's thrilled enough to go and
                                tell your tale.

Millions of people are confined in quite possibly the smallest of spaces. And at the precipice of it all, not one foothill glances upward, into mountains, where a cliff is simply a shoulder.

If any one thing is to be considered funny, well, then, *everything* could be funny; although, this must be the least "funny" of all things—not necessarily overwhelming, yet certainly not underwhelming—but serious grimacing going on inside an Indian restaurant.

Appropriate levels of specialty; (keeping in mind off-putting eccentricities) but it's not common for anyone to be vaguely anything.

Half of what you is, isn't, but if you isn't, surely, you could be, if that just *happens* to be true.

Realistic, intrinsic qualities are making up a large quantity of space inside my brain. Every neuron is firing in succession, then inside my dishonest possession lies the fallacy that imbeds itself into my sturdy bones.

Negativity hasn't gotten me very far (so far) and that's the truth. Yet, I cling to what is "realistic" for the sake of unexciting my youth. But, if keeping myself "in touch" with what's real is denying all that I cannot feel, then I absolutely do not seek it. Of course, I can't help but attempt to aid the possibility of pain by replacing it with precursors. Has hope become extinct in this world of stagnant social-classes? Supposedly, no! But believably, yes! I can't help but feel alone in these diverse environments constructed to include me. Doesn't this perpetuate the exact issue? And does it, indeed, confirm the motionlessness of our class structure? Or does it mean all this is just totally in my head? Am I feeling or am I perceiving, here? Does altering your socioeconomic status necessitate a complete upheaval of any perception of yourself?

Perhaps the majority of what creates these so-called "classes" is just in all our heads. The wolf-in-sheep's-clothing concept, in this sense, is just a sheep that failed to recognize itself as a sheep. So, is it possible, then that the concept of immoveable social classes had been invented by the unmotivated in order to perpetuate the ultimately unmotivated? Sure, it is! What may be real or true or honest (which turns out to be subjective) is that pessimism won't be a good fit for this "funny" world.

There's just too much to be happy about to be spoiled by three rather upsetting things. Think of these three steps instead: (1) what you dream about coming into supposed fruition. (2) Aiming for the sky and inventing a safety net, all the while pretending to be a skydiver. (3) In a way, forming your own reality and, therefore, shaping yourself, molding into carved crutches, holding the strict curvature.

All this being said, I'm guessing that one doesn't, simply, surrender. Of course not! One truly never knows when that lightening bolt stroke of luck is immanent.

IN A SEASON OF NEVERENDING TIME

Grey as the sky, as the sky is blue:
Myself as the one, who's the one for you;
Among crystalline pillars, I watch this room,
And time is never ending as the
                    spindle breaks anew.

As the fuzz fucks hard
And the weeds whack lightly:
Pistol shots fire,
As the sun comes nightly.

Terrible things arise
As a bitter wind falls,
So death shall turn miraculously,
Until the end is stalled.

Flowers bundled: the coolidge;
Stems cut, uprooted;
Buds blend on borderlines;
Petals fall: an overdue demise.

Waiting is the hardest part
As fear flies, and zings, and darts
Right into your soft flesh
Keep on waiting, mind—to rest!

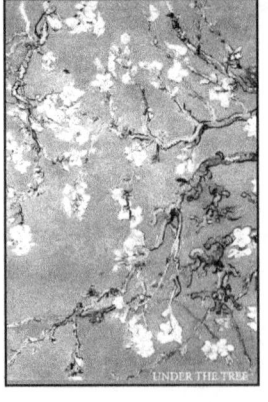

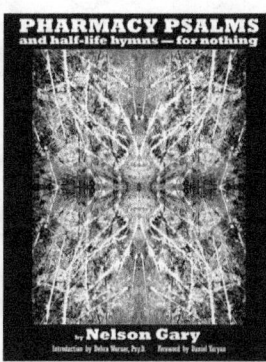

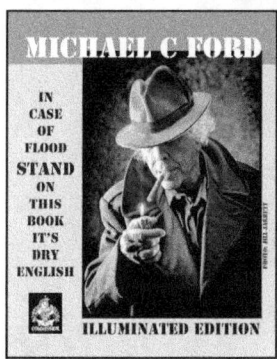
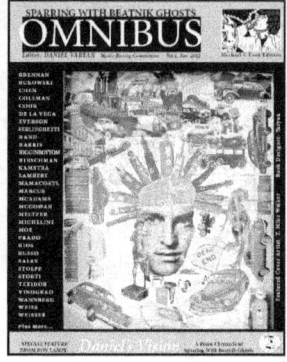

Under the Tree:
The Tree Academy
Anthology
of Poetry &
Prose...

Available at:
www.*sparringartists.com*